D0810200

Also by Nancy Ruth Patterson

The Winner's Walk

A Simple Gift

The Shiniest Rock of All

The Christmas Cup

Ellie Ever

Nancy Ruth Patterson

Pictures by Patty Weise

Farrar Straus Giroux • New York

www.fsgkidsbooks.com

Library of Congress Cataloging-in-Publication Data
Patterson, Nancy Ruth.
    Ellie Ever / Nancy Ruth Patterson ; pictures by Patty Weise.— 1st ed.
        p.   cm.
    Summary: After losing her father and all their possessions in a
hurricane, nine-year-old Ellie and her mother move to a small
apartment on a horse farm in Virginia, where her new classmates
think that she lives in a mansion and is a princess.
    ISBN: 978-0-374-32108-6
    [1. Rumor—Fiction.   2. Conduct of life—Fiction.   3. Horses—
Fiction.]   I. Weise, Patty, ill.   II. Title.

PZ7.P27814El 2010
[Fic]—dc22

                                                        2009013604

For my aunt, Mary Lou McCune King,
and her very special Kingdom,
and,
as always, for my mother,
Willeyne McCune Clemens

Ever!

—N.R.P.

1

Ellie Taylor hated it when people called her and the other kids heroes.

"Heroes in hand-me-downs," the church lady giving out sweaters to the children in the homeless shelter said to nobody in particular on Christmas Eve. Ellie wondered how that fake honor could make anybody who'd lost just about everything they had in a "natural disaster" feel better.

Ellie knew full well she wasn't a hero because a hateful hurricane had swallowed her house. It had washed away the shutters and doors and kitchen sink. It had also washed away whole neighborhoods and even managed to kidnap her beloved Saint

Bernard, Pandy. But just surviving a hurricane didn't make her a hero.

A hero was somebody who'd done something special, something important, something unselfish. Somebody like her father, who had drowned trying to rescue people afterwards.

Her mother knew they weren't heroes, and they weren't "victims" either, like the TV said, or "homeless people." Her mother really hated that one.

"We're just between homes," her mother had said. " '*Tweeners*. Let's call ourselves '*tweeners*."

'*Tweeners* sounded so much more hopeful to Ellie than *homeless*.

The used sweaters and sweatshirts had been donated for children the hurricane had left homeless. When the church lady turned her back, one of the bigger kids tried to take two sweaters from one of the boxes.

"Remember, one per customer," she said kindly as she turned around and saw him. "There are so many other children who need them, too. Why, I'm going to another shelter as soon as I leave here. We need to save some for those children."

The boy sheepishly put one sweater back.

It was Ellie's turn to rummage through the giveaway box labeled MEDIUM in search of a sweater that would fit a nine-year-old.

Ellie spied one she thought would be perfect for Christmas. True, the neck had been stretched to the size of a soup bowl, and the sleeves hung an inch below her fingertips. But it was bright red, and it looked like it would keep her warm. Best of all, it had a basset hound wearing a silly Santa hat woven into the front. Just perfect for an animal lover like me, Ellie thought. She thanked the lady politely and turned to leave.

But as she turned, she spotted a puffy little face in the pile. She reached in and pulled out a reindeer sweater with a soft red nose fashioned from yarn. It was too big for her, but the perfect size for her mom. And a reindeer looked a little bit like a horse, she figured. She wondered if reindeer wore horseshoes. Horseshoes like the ones her father used to make when he was alive and had his farrier business, Taylor-Made Horseshoes. Horseshoes like the ones her mother kept saying she wanted to make someday.

But the church lady had said one to a customer.

Ellie started to walk away; then she decided she'd rather have the one with the fuzzy-nosed reindeer. It would be a perfect Christmas present for her mom. She went to the back of the line and waited while the children in front of her each picked a sweater. She hoped nobody else would like the reindeer sweater as much as she did.

Beth, who lived in the room next to theirs at the shelter, patted the red yarn of the reindeer's nose, then put it back. "It's too big for you," the lady told her, handing her a snowman sweatshirt instead. Beth sprinted out of the room, smiling.

As the line inched its way shorter and shorter, Ellie felt her heart beat faster and faster. She thought—she hoped—that the last three boys would want the Dallas Cowboys sweatshirts that she had seen in the box, not the reindeer sweater. Ellie felt relieved when they grabbed them and began to run around the room throwing imaginary touchdowns.

"Haven't I seen you before?" the church lady asked when Ellie reached the boxes.

Ellie looked at the sweater she wanted for her mother. She tickled the reindeer's nose tenderly.

"You really like this one, don't you?" the lady

asked. "It's one of my favorites, too. As a matter of fact, it was mine once, until I outgrew it." She patted her stomach playfully. "I thought one of the older, larger children might like it. It must have gotten mixed up in the box of sweaters for younger kids."

"I was just wondering if maybe, if possibly I could trade this one"—Ellie held out her basset hound sweater—"for the reindeer one?"

"But it's way too big for you," said the lady, holding it up to Ellie's shoulders. "See, it's even big enough for your mother."

Ellie looked down.

"Is that why you want it? It is, isn't it? You want a Christmas present for your mother."

Ellie nodded. She had heard that the church ladies who volunteered at the shelter would have special presents for children spending Christmas there, but Ellie wanted something special for her mother, too. She folded her basset hound sweater neatly and put it back in the box.

"Tell you what," the lady said. "If you won't tell the other kids, you can have them both."

"Wouldn't be fair," Ellie said. "You said one per customer."

"Well, everybody sure left these boxes in a mess. I saw how neatly you folded your sweater just now." The lady looked into Ellie's eyes. "I've got a great idea," she said. "Why don't you help me fold the rest of these sweaters and make sure they are in the right boxes according to size. Then you can take a second sweater. That would be fair. We'll consider it your paycheck."

Ellie hesitated.

"I could really use your help," the lady said convincingly. "I'm already late to my next stop."

Ellie spent fifteen minutes folding sweaters and sweatshirts and putting them in the boxes marked SMALL, MEDIUM, and LARGE. Then she helped the church lady take the three boxes out to her car.

Ellie raced back to her room with both the reindeer sweater and the basset hound one. She hid the reindeer sweater under her blanket.

Now she would have something to give her mother tomorrow morning.

For the first time, Ellie had a feeling that this Christmas might turn out to be pretty good after all.

Ellie woke up Christmas morning in Noah's Ark, which was the name on the door of the Taylors' room in the homeless shelter. Run by a church, this shelter was their home between homes, her mother had explained when they moved in that fall. It was much nicer than the overcrowded gym where they had slept on cots and showered in a locker room for a month after the hurricane.

She and her mother had become the first residents of the dozen studio apartments converted from unused Sunday School classrooms to house kids and their families temporarily. Ellie's mom had told her she could pick out their apartment, and Ellie had chosen the one with a mural of Noah's Ark on one wall. In its previous life, the apartment had been the church nursery. Ellie gave each of the animals on the deck of the ark in the mural a name and tried to learn every fact about them from an old encyclopedia in the church library. She wanted to be a veterinarian when she grew up, and she thought the knowledge might come in handy.

Besides, seeing Noah and the animals on his ark gave Ellie hope that someone like Noah had rescued Pandy. Pandy had been recuperating from surgery at an animal hospital across town when the threat of a hurricane forced them to evacuate. Her mother had tried to pick Pandy up before they fled, but she couldn't fight the bumper-to-bumper traffic. "Your father will join us with Pandy after he helps with the evacuation," her mother had said. But her father never came. The animal hospital had been flooded, and nobody seemed to know what had happened to the veterinarian, let alone the animals in his care.

Ellie knew this Christmas would be different from the ones they had spent in their old home.

Just last Christmas her father had helped her make ornaments for their extra-tall spruce tree. Ellie had cut out pictures of animals from a magazine, and he had varnished them onto small circles of balsa wood. When the varnish was dry, her mother had poked red and green ribbons through the holes drilled in the top of the ornaments, and Pandy had barked when Ellie tied them on the tree.

"We probably have the only tree in America with a polar bear, a platypus, and a prairie dog," her father had said.

Ellie knew the hurricane had stolen those ornaments, too, but she tried not to think about it. Instead, she thought of their Christmas traditions that would stay the same.

Fried chicken and waffles for breakfast! That Taylor Christmas tradition would be the same, her mother had promised. Mrs. Taylor had a temporary job every weekday morning as a short-order cook in town, and she also cooked for the shelter on weekends and holidays. "Earning our keep," she called it. Everybody at the shelter looked forward to her mother's cooking, and Ellie felt sure they would love the Taylor tradition of fried chicken and waffles for Christmas breakfast.

Ellie peeked under the cover to be sure her

mother's secret gift was still safe. Then she brushed her teeth, smoothed her hair as best she could, pulled on her basset hound sweater and jeans, and headed to the dining room. She could hear some of the children who had already gathered shrieking with delight, the smell of frying chicken thick in the air.

Miss Helen Beckwith, who had come out of retirement to volunteer at the shelter, was wearing a Santa hat and ho-ho-ho-ing hugs at the door. Ellie saw at once why the other kids were shrieking. Packages of every size and shape circled the artificial tree. Ellie counted sixteen packages—one for every child. She could tell from its shape that one package was a skateboard—probably for a kid named Jason, who talked about skateboarding all the time. A handlebar had punctured the paper on another package, a bike, for sure. Mike Stanley had asked for that, and she hoped it was his. A small package peeked out of a velvet stocking hanging on the tree. She wondered what could possibly be that tiny. The tags on the packages were turned so that the names didn't show. Ellie wondered which one would have her name.

Ellie's mom announced that breakfast could wait. She would keep it warm in the oven while the kids saw what Santa had left. One by one, Miss Beckwith called their names. One by one, the children exclaimed that Santa had left exactly what they had asked for. Then Miss Beckwith handed each adult a big box of chocolates.

She left Ellie's package, the tiny one peeking from the stocking, for last. "You might want to wait until you're alone with your mother to open it," Miss Beckwith whispered to her. Ellie couldn't imagine what was in the package. Oh, she had written the letter Miss Beckwith had asked them to write, but it couldn't be that. What she had asked for in that letter couldn't be wrapped up and tied with a bow. She could hardly wait to finish her fried chicken and syrup-drenched waffles to find out what was inside.

When they were back at Noah's Ark, Ellie gave her mother the sweater. "It's so cute," Mrs. Taylor exclaimed, pinching the reindeer's nose, then Ellie's. "Now it's your turn, Ellie."

Ellie sat on the side of her cot, prying the paper off the little box while her mother sat beside her,

smiling. "You already know what's in it, don't you?" Ellie asked. Her mother smiled bigger.

In the box was a piece of folded stationery.

Ellie began to read the letter.

Dear Ellie,

My name is Charles Beckwith. Helen Beckwith is my sister. She sent me the letters all the children at the shelter had written so that I could help Santa find the right gift for everyone. Most of the children's wishes were easy to find, but your Christmas wishes were a little harder to come by.

Santa said in his whole career no other child had ever asked him to help her mother become a farrier.

We checked with your mother to be sure that she really did want to shoe horses. Then we went to work.

I remembered that a college roommate of mine, Jake Hunter, had just purchased a large farm in Virginia horse country. His hobby is rescuing horses whose owners think are too old or too lame or too sick to keep. He wants those horses to live out their lives in the green pastures of his new farm. But because he and his wife spend winters at their Florida home, he needs somebody to live on the farm to take care of the horses. The great news is that he has offered the job to your mother, who has agreed to start work January 1. The job at the horse farm will only take a few hours a day, allowing her to work as an apprentice to one of the best farriers in Virginia, who lives nearby.

Mr. Hunter regrets that he will be unable to meet you in January. He'll be returning to the farm in April. Meanwhile, the farm manager, Grover Cook, will stay on long enough to show you and your mother around. He'll be retiring after you're settled in.

My sister told me about your father's heroism. She also wrote me that the principal at the school you've been attending told her you are one of the best students she has ever seen. My sister convinced me that you deserve a truly fine education. Twin Creeks Preparatory School, one of the most prestigious private girls' schools in the country, is not too far from the Hunters' estate. I asked your mother to send the headmaster there copies of your report cards and test scores. Because of your remarkable academic gifts, the school is pleased to award you a full scholarship for as long as you live near Twin Creeks and keep up your excellent grades. My sister and I know you will excel there.

I wish I could tell you that Santa's helpers had located your dog, Pandy, whom you also mentioned in your letter. My sister forwarded me a copy of the picture you showed her. As you may know, thousands of dogs were rescued during the hurricane, and many of them are still waiting for their owners at shelters across the country. We will continue to do what we can to help find Pandy.

Merry Christmas, Ellie. I hope this letter comes as good tidings in response to your Christmas wish.

Most sincerely,

Charles Beckwith

Ellie had never seen the word *tidings* before, but she was pretty sure the letter meant that her mother had a job with the prospect of an even better job when she learned to shoe horses. Ellie knew her father had made a nice living as a farrier. Why couldn't her mother become the Taylor in Taylor-Made Horseshoes? She could almost picture her father smiling.

She was pretty sure that *good tidings* also meant they wouldn't be 'tweeners anymore—that they wouldn't have to worry so much about spending the last of the small insurance settlement her father had left them, and pretty soon they might even have enough money to buy a new house.

Her mother hugged Ellie tight. The reindeer's nose on her sweater poked Ellie, and she found herself giggling and crying at the same time.

Ellie thought the whole world smelled wonderful again, even better than fried chicken and waffles.

3

What kind of people live in places like these?" Ellie asked as they wound their way past all the sprawling horse farms en route to the Hunters' estate. Sometimes she could see gigantic houses behind the white fences. Sometimes an enormous gate hinted at the size of the house it protected.

"Rich ones, I suppose," her mother said.

"These people don't have neighbors, at least not ones I can see. They can't just run next door to borrow a cup of sugar like we used to do."

"Not unless they're long-distance runners. This must be where we turn."

"It's the biggest house I've ever seen!" Ellie said as the Blue Goose rolled to a stop in front of a massive iron gate. The Blue Goose, their truck, was almost like part of the family. Her father had called it his office on wheels, the only office he ever needed for visiting his customers. They affectionately called it the Blue Goose because of the goose-honking sound of its horn, and when her mother honked at the gate, Ellie recalled that she could not remember a day when she hadn't heard that goose-honk at least once. She was glad her mother had driven away from the hurricane in the Blue Goose instead of using their old Chevy, even though the memory of her father at the wheel still made her sad.

Before Mrs. Taylor could find the right button to punch on the intercom, the gate opened up. The Blue Goose began to bounce over the cattle guards embedded into the sides of a shallow pit.

"Is *that* where we're going to live?" Ellie exclaimed as she eyed the mansion at the end of the long driveway.

"Just who do you think you are?" her mother asked, laughing.

As the Blue Goose pulled to a stop, a grizzly of a man in khakis and a heavy green jacket waved

them to a spot on the circular driveway. Ellie and her mom got out of the truck. He lumbered toward them. "Looks like you made it," the man said. "I'm Grover Cook, the farm manager." Ellie thought his voice sounded gruff.

"I'm Annie Taylor, and this is my daughter, Ellie."

Mr. Cook shook Ellie's mom's hand before taking Ellie's tiny hand in his big, calloused one.

"Glad to meet you both," he said.

"Have you worked here long?" Mrs. Taylor asked.

"About forty years for the former owners, the Angles. They sold the place to Mr. Hunter a few months ago. I told him I'd stay on for a while, until he found somebody to take my place. Now that you're here, my wife and I will be taking off for California in the RV the Angles gave us."

Ellie looked at two workers straining to carry a long slab of gray granite into the mansion. "The Hunters are having the house renovated while they are in Florida for the winter," Mr. Cook explained, "though if you ask me, the place looked just fine the way the Angles left it."

Ellie wondered where they would be living and what their house would look like. It had to be bigger than Noah's Ark. Maybe about the size of her house B.H.—that's what her mother called the time Before the Hurricane.

"Looks like you've come well-equipped," Mr. Cook said, peering into the window of the metal enclosure that tented the truck's bed. Without even looking, Ellie knew what he would see: a few cardboard boxes of personal items; racks loaded with metal shoes in different shapes and sizes; hoof rasps for filing; big pliers called clinchers; a few hammers; an anvil heavy with scars; her father's well-worn leather apron; and, best of all, a gas forge that breathed fire—the Dragon, her father had nicknamed it. Her father had joked that a farrier only needed three things to go into business: something to hammer, something to hammer with, and something to hammer on. The Blue Goose, bulging with the latest in footwear for the well-shod horse, proved otherwise.

"You're smaller than I imagined," Mr. Cook said to Mrs. Taylor. "Smaller than most farriers, I mean."

It was true, Ellie thought. But somehow she had never thought of her mother as small, and her mother wouldn't let something like being short stand in the way of a challenge. She didn't make excuses for herself, and she didn't like anybody else's excuses either.

"I've got a way with horses," Mrs. Taylor said confidently. "They don't seem to mind that I'm small. My husband used to say that every horse I meet falls in love with me at first sight, just like he did."

"Wrestling with a horse that doesn't want to wear shoes can be awfully hard," Mr. Cook warned. "Do you know what you're getting yourself into?" He sounded doubtful.

She nodded. "I'm a novice, but I watched farriers work on the farm where I grew up. Sometimes I'd go out to the stables to watch my husband shoe, hand him tools, that sort of thing. I wish he had taught me more, but we never thought . . ." She didn't finish her statement.

"The Angles wouldn't have had a novice shoeing horses around here, that's for sure. Not that it matters much anymore."

Ellie wondered why it didn't matter much anymore. She wished Mr. Cook would stop talking that way to her mother.

"This place used to be one of the best stables

anywhere when the Angles owned it. A winner in every stall. Now it's just a stable of"—Mr. Cook paused, groping for the word he wanted—"of misfits."

"I think we'll like it here just fine," her mother said.

"Well, you must be anxious to settle in—with school starting for you both tomorrow."

Ellie hadn't really thought of her mother's beginning her job as a farrier's apprentice being the same as starting school.

"I need to get the keys from the house before I take you to your apartment," Mr. Cook said. "You all can come in and look around if you like."

Ellie stood just inside the doorway gawking at the massive mahogany spiral staircase. She could hear hammering and sawing on the second floor and smell varnish on newly refinished hardwood floors. The varnish smell reminded her of her dad and of the tree ornaments they had made B.H.

Mr. Cook retrieved the keys from a small hook in the coat closet and then stooped to pick up a package resting on the bottom step of the staircase.

"Here's a package for you from that school you'll be attending," he said.

Ellie glanced at the distinguished-looking return address.

TWIN CREEKS
PREPARATORY SCHOOL
Twin Creeks, Virginia

"Don't worry, Ellie. You can't already be in trouble," he said a little more softly, handing her the package. "You haven't even started school yet."

Mr. Cook ushered them toward their truck. "I better show you where you'll be living. Follow my van."

Ellie and her mother climbed back into the Blue Goose.

"I don't think he likes us," Ellie said as they bounced their way over cobblestones toward the stable.

"He just doesn't like that everything is changing. His bark is probably worse than his bite."

The Blue Goose bucked into second gear.

"I think your father would be proud of us," Mrs. Taylor said.

Ellie's heart wrinkled at the mention of her father. She remembered what her mother had told her after her father died. "We Taylors are strong stock," she had said time and time again. "We don't stay down, and we don't stay out. And we don't let our hearts stay broken forever. Wrinkled, maybe, but never broken."

So Ellie and her wrinkled heart bounced along a bumpy road all the way to their new home.

4

Their new home wasn't exactly what Ellie had been expecting. Mr. Cook unlocked the door to a small building painted light blue and white—a miniature replica of the handsome stables a few hundred feet down the hill. There was a horse-shaped weathervane on the roof—just like the one that sat on the stable roof—and a horseshoe-shaped knocker on the door. He handed the keys to Mrs. Taylor and ushered them into a room still thick with the smell of fresh-cut wood. "Your living room used to be my office," he explained. "Makes a nice apartment, if I do say so myself."

Ellie wound her way through their quarters, which the carpenters had renovated before they started on the Hunters' house. She pulled her mother along by the hand. Mr. Cook turned on a light sprouting from the head of a porcelain horse. A warm glow settled over a well-worn leather sofa and two overstuffed club chairs in the living room next to the tiny galley kitchen. Ellie ran toward one of three small windows that overlooked the paddock, where two horses stood quietly, the bay resting his dark brown head on the buckskin's tan withers.

"Say hello to your neighbors," Mr. Cook said.

Mrs. Taylor opened the window and made clicking sounds to get the horses' attention.

Both horses looked up and neighed at the same time as if to welcome Ellie and her mother to the neighborhood.

"Glory, the brown one, is really old, forty years, maybe more, though it's hard to tell exactly because he's lost most of his teeth. They tell me he used to run with the best of them, but now . . ."

"He'll like the soft molasses mash I'll make him. An old family recipe." Mrs. Taylor smiled. "The buckskin's good-looking."

"That's Buttermilk. She splintered the pastern

of her left hind leg a year ago. You can't tell by the way she's standing now, but she's real limpy."

"What about that one, Mr. Cook?" Ellie asked. She pointed to a pinkish-colored horse, a roan, two hands shorter and a whole lot stockier than the other horses. "He's really beautiful."

"From one side, maybe. Wait till he turns around. His name is Pogo. He was burned in a stable fire in Connecticut over Thanksgiving. His left shoulder's still one big scab. They tried to get him out of the fire, but he was so scared he ran back into the stable, where he thought he'd be safe. If they'd just have put blinders, even a wet rag, over his eyes . . ."

Ellie winced. "What about that one? What's that horse's name?"

"Hannibal. Got into a corn crib and foundered. Founder's a bad inflammation of the hoof. It's real painful for the horse," he explained, looking at El-lie. "The vets did what they could, but his owner discovered the problem too late."

Ellie hoped she would be able to cure horses like Hannibal when she became a veterinarian.

"What about the horse way off in the pasture? The one all by himself?"

"That mustang? Outlaw. Can't get anywhere near him. Nobody can. Wildest horse I've seen in a long time. A trainer—if you can call him that, and I can't say I would—cracked Outlaw between the ears with a two-by-four when he reared up at him. You can still see the scar. Hasn't trusted a human since. He's a biter. Kicker, too. Got to keep him by himself. Took four of us to load him in the trailer and bring him here. I'm still sore from where he kicked me." He rubbed his right leg.

"What about that pony?"

"Raffles. Mr. Hunter said his daughter won her in a drawing twenty-five years ago. She'd paid five dollars for the winning ticket. Said she was so proud of her prize that he didn't have the heart to tell her the filly was overpriced, even at that." He laughed. "Said his daughter proved him wrong. Won the national three-day event with her. I guess you never know how things will turn out."

"Is something wrong with Raffles?" Ellie was almost afraid to ask.

"Her owner grew too old for her, that's all. And she's up in years."

"I'm glad he's rescued them all," Mrs. Taylor said. "We'll take good care of them."

"On nice days we let them out in the paddock all day for exercise, but they stay in their stalls at night," Mr. Cook said. "All except Outlaw. We drop his food off in the shed at the corner of his pasture and let him come to it when he's good and ready. Remember to check his water, make sure it's not frozen. And he likes salt."

"I'll remember to check," Mrs. Taylor said.

"Could I learn to ride on any of them?" Ellie asked. She had wanted to learn for a long time.

"Not here. They're all too old or too lame or too wild."

"Can I pet them?"

"Sure can, if they'll let you. Except for Outlaw. I wouldn't try to pet him unless you'd like a hoof-print for a tattoo. Don't you want to see the rest of the place?" he asked them, changing the subject.

Across the hall, Ellie saw a bedroom. Painted a pale blue, it had photographs of jumping horses on every wall and a white spread over the double bed.

"I guess you're wondering where your room is," Mr. Cook said to Ellie. "See those stairs?" He pointed toward one corner of the bedroom. Ellie's mom and Mr. Cook followed as she bounded up the stairs two at a time. Ellie's loft hung over her mother's room, blocked off only by a sturdy rail. It was handsome in a horsy sort of way: a colorful patchwork quilt covering a white iron bed; horse pictures all over the wall; even a rocking chair with a horse's head carved into the top. Beside the bed, a lamp seemed to grow out of a tall riding boot.

"Everything's great!" Ellie exclaimed. She wished she could think of a better word, but surprise had shocked the better words right out of her head.

When they all went back downstairs, Ellie's mother went out to the Blue Goose and came back with the package from her new school. "Aren't you going to open it?" she asked.

Ellie pried open the box. A handbook of rules. White blouses with little round collars monogrammed *TCPS*. Tartan-plaid skirts. A navy blazer with a brightly colored emblem.

"I got a letter from the school just before Christmas, asking about your size. They wear uniforms there," her mother said. "I like that idea. You never have to wonder what to wear."

Ellie was glad they'd all be dressing the same. She had outgrown the few clothes she had taken from home when they evacuated, and there hadn't been money to buy new ones.

"You ought to see those girls strut around town in their uniforms," Mr. Cook said. "Acting like they own the place. Scratch any one of them and you'll sniff a snob."

"Sniff a snob, and you'll get a whiff of scared," Mrs. Taylor said. "Besides, all the girls can't be like that. You probably just ran into a few bad ones."

"Hope *you* don't turn out that way," Mr. Cook said to Ellie.

Ellie had never met a real snob before, but she knew she would never be one. "I won't. I promise."

"She better not, if she knows what's good for her," Mrs. Taylor said, shaking her finger playfully at Ellie.

"What about shoes?" Ellie asked. "I wonder what kind of shoes they wear at"—she stuttered the letters out—"at T-C-P-S?"

"Maybe it says in the handbook," her mother suggested.

Ellie quickly thumbed through the pages.

"It says either black or brown. No high heels. No tennis shoes."

Ellie knew she had the perfect shoes carefully packed away in the Blue Goose.

5

Mr. Cook insisted on carrying all the heavy boxes himself. Then he took the rest of the afternoon to show Mrs. Taylor just how things should be done at Hunters' Hill. When he was finished, he wished Ellie and her mother good luck and walked out to the paddock.

"Come here, Ellie," her mother said after he had left.

Ellie stood beside her mother, sneaking a look out the window from behind the curtain.

Mr. Cook walked around the paddock, glancing up as if to be sure nobody was watching. He stopped to nuzzle each horse—except, of course, Outlaw. He head-rubbed some, shoulder-patted others. He took a chunk of carrot from his coat pocket, dropped it in a bucket, and set it on the ground in front of Pogo.

"Mr. Cook's bark *is* worse than his bite," Ellie said.

"Most barks are," Mrs. Taylor agreed.

Ellie climbed the stairs to her loft, carefully pried off the top of the box her mother had labeled ELLIE'S VALUABLES, and stacked each valuable in a neat pile at the foot of her new bed. She knew her valuables weren't as great as the ones in the box of valuables labeled with her mother's name. That box had family pictures and the old family Bible. It had a letter from their governor calling her father a true American hero for trying to evacuate people after the hurricane.

Ellie opened her box and thumbed through pieces of her own history:

— all her report cards (*straight A's*; *works well with others*; *perfect scores on the state test*; *needs to practice her penmanship*);

— the photograph of her old soccer team (*third from left, next to her best*

*friend, Emma; Most Improved Player
trophy sitting on her lap);*

— her baby book (*light brown curl from
her first haircut; favorite toy—Leroy
the Lion; favorite song—"Wheels
on the Bus"*);

— the shoes (*black patent leather ballet
flats with a bow; wrapped in a velvet
shoe bag*)

Ellie cradled the shoes in her palms, slipped the
left one over her fingers like a hand puppet, then
rubbed a fingerprint from the leather. She tried it
on. At last—it fit!

They'll dress up that old-fashioned uniform, she
thought.

"Mom, will you tell me the shoe story again?"
Ellie called over the rails of her loft bedroom. "I
think I've forgotten *exactly* what Daddy said when
he bought them for me." She could remember perfectly well, but she loved hearing her mom tell the
story.

"Oh, Ellie Taylor. We've got so much unpacking
to do." Ellie thought her mother sounded tired. "And

I haven't fed the horses yet. Besides, you've heard that story at least a million times. You know it better than I do."

"But I can't remember *exactly* anymore," Ellie said. Her mother kept on unpacking. "Maybe I could help you feed the horses." Ellie changed the subject. She knew it was not a good time to beg.

"Well, go see if you can find the halters and the leads," her mother said, hanging a crisp blouse and some blue jeans in the closet. "I'll try to bribe the horses into their stalls with some corn."

"Do you remember all their names?" Ellie asked.

"There's Glory and Buttermilk, Hannibal and Pogo, Outlaw and Ruffles."

"Raffles, Mom. Not Ruffles. Remember how Mr. Hunter's daughter won Raffles in a drawing?"

Her mother nodded. "Raffles."

A little later, Ellie and her mom went outside, and Ellie stood at the paddock gate watching as her mother made friends with the horses Mr. Cook had called misfits. All of them—well, all except Outlaw—seemed to trust her right away, Ellie thought proudly. Horses really did fall in love with her mother at first sight, just the way her father had said! One by one, Mrs. Taylor led each horse back into its stall.

Then her mother pitched hay into the hayracks and measured grain into the troughs. She mixed warm water into Glory's senior feed, smashing it soft enough for the old horse to gum. Tomorrow, she promised him, she would make him some special mash.

"Want to walk with me to feed Outlaw?" she asked Ellie. "I'll tell you that story on the way there." The sun was setting winter orange as they walked down to the pasture.

"It was a few weeks before the hurricane," Ellie's mom began, "and your father had taken you and me to eat lunch at a fancy French restaurant."

"And I ordered French fries because it was the only French food I'd ever heard of," Ellie added.

"You did order French fries," her mother said, nodding. "After lunch, we were walking back to where we had parked the Blue Goose when you spied a pair of black patent leather ballet flats in the window of a boutique for children."

"*Boutique* is the French word for store," Ellie reminded her mother. "A very expensive store."

"It was a very expensive store," her mother agreed. "But that didn't stop your father. He didn't even ask how much the shoes cost when he took you in to try them on, though he knew perfectly well that we couldn't afford them."

"Did you ask how much they cost?"

"Of course," her mother said. "Someone in the family had to be sensible, and your father never was when it came to you. He spoiled you rotten."

"Really rotten?" Ellie knew the answer, but she wanted her mother to say it.

"Rottenest of the rotten," her mother said. "Not only did the shoes cost five times as much as a perfectly good pair would cost where we usually shopped, but the store didn't even have a pair that fit you. The ones you had fallen in love with were a size too big!"

"And Dad said that I'd grow into them one day."

"He did say that, didn't he?" She smiled at Ellie. "I knew it wouldn't do any good to argue with him," her mother said softly, shaking her head in pretend disapproval. "Those way-too-expensive, too-big black patent leather shoes already had your name on them!"

"And that night, when he tucked me in, I asked him if my new shoes were as good as his Taylor-Made shoes."

"You did indeed."

"And he said, 'Well, *almost* as good.'" Ellie tried to imitate her father's low voice.

"Yes. That's what he said—*almost* as good!"

"Almost as good as Taylor-Made shoes," Ellie said proudly, trying to keep up with her mother's stride.

Mrs. Taylor left a bucket of sweet feed for Outlaw and scattered a hunk of hay that she had carried there in a burlap bag. Then she checked his water and block of salt.

"You think anybody could ever tame Outlaw?" Ellie asked as they walked away.

"If the right person tried, I wouldn't be surprised."

"How would the right person start?" Ellie asked.

"By changing his name," her mother said. "How would you liked to be called Outlaw?"

"Can you change a horse's name?"

"I'm sure Outlaw wouldn't mind, and I don't see anybody else around here to tell us not to. Think of a good name for him, Ellie, something wonderful.

But don't you *dare* go near him when I'm not with you, you hear me?"

Ellie knew her mother meant business when she used that tone of voice.

"I'll just think of a name from a distance," Ellie said as they went inside for a supper of the pot roast and green beans and chocolate pie that Mr. Cook's wife had left in their refrigerator that morning.

Ellie had a hard time falling asleep the first night in their new house. So much for her to think about. What would TCPS be like? Would she be as smart as the other girls there? Would she have friends? Would there be bullies? Probably not, Ellie thought. Girls wouldn't be bullies, would they? But what about snobs?

Most of all, she kept thinking about Mr. Hunter. She had never heard of anybody like him before. He could probably buy any horse he wanted, but instead he had brought a whole stable of what Mr. Cook had called misfits to live at Hunters' Hill. She herself would never call them misfits, that was for sure.

"I know, Mom. Let's name him Pandora," Ellie yelled through the darkness to her mother. Pandora was her dog Pandy's real name.

"That's a girl's name. Now go to sleep."

"How about Pandemonium? That's what Dad called Pandy sometimes."

"That word means chaos, Ellie. Your father was teasing when he called your dog that. Now go to sleep."

"How about Okey? As in Okey Dokey," Ellie suggested. "Dad used to say 'okey dokey' all the time." Ellie remembered her father's deep voice saying that. Not "okay" or "fine," like other fathers said, always "okey dokey."

"Go to sleep, Ellie. It's almost tomorrow."

"Okey dokey," she said.

The last thing Ellie remembered before drifting off was seeing the almost-as-good-as-Taylor-Made shoes standing at attention beside her bed.

6

Alphabetical order! Mrs. Crispin said her fourth grade had to sit in alphabetical order—just like the other fourth-grade classes she had taught for forty-two years at Twin Creeks Prep. She sat Ellie Taylor in the row next to the window right between Chloe Sampson and Hannah Williams, who definitely acted like best friends. If she could have, Ellie would have traded places with Hannah so the two friends could still sit together the way they wanted to, but she bet nobody had ever defied Mrs. Crispin's rules.

Of the sixteen girls in Mrs. Crispin's class, fifteen already knew one another. Ellie could feel thirty eyes, not counting Mrs. Crispin's, staring at her as she stood by her desk and said her name.

"Ellie Taylor," she mumbled quietly.

Mrs. Crispin peered from behind an extra-large pair of tortoiseshell glasses. "Now say your name again, young lady—only this time louder, as if you are *proud* of it."

Ellie felt her face flush. "Elizabeth Ever Taylor," she said again, this time in the loudest indoor voice she could muster. "Everybody calls me Ellie."

Mrs. Crispin walked toward Ellie and pulled back gently on her shoulders. "Stand up straight," she commanded.

Ellie could feel the slouchiness straighten under Mrs. Crispin's bony hands. Then Mrs. Crispin cradled Ellie's chin in her palm and lifted it uncomfortably high. She thought she heard someone behind her start to giggle, but the giggle stopped as quickly as it started.

"My girls always keep their heads high and their shoulders squared," Mrs. Crispin said. "And they always say their names *proudly*.

"Ellie Taylor is one of three girls new to Twin

Creeks second semester," Mrs. Crispin said as she walked to the front of the room, "but she is the only new girl in the fourth grade. I know you'll make her feel welcome. Now please stand and introduce yourself to Ellie."

One by one, each of the girls stood by her desk, straightened her shoulders, and said her name proudly.

Ellie thought some of the first names sounded strange—like last names—McGregor Adams, for example, and Kennedy Cartright. She was glad they all dressed in the same old-fashioned uniforms. She wondered if anybody had noticed her shoes yet. They were so much prettier than the plain brown ones most of the other girls wore.

"Now let's see how much you forgot over the holidays," Mrs. Crispin said. She moved a wheel—kind of like the one Ellie had seen on *Wheel of Fortune*—in front of her desk and gave it a spin. Slips of paper containing review questions from first semester were taped by each number, and they fluttered when the pointer on the wheel whizzed by. "When you know the answer to the question, raise your hand."

Mrs. Crispin's mood seemed to brighten every time Ellie raised her hand to answer a question. "384 divided by 24?"

"Sixteen."

Mrs. Crispin gave the wheel another spin.

"Year Jamestown was founded?"

"1607."

"That's correct, Ellie."

Another spin.

"Second president of the United States?"

Ellie raised her hand for that one, too.

"John Adams."

Mrs. Crispin smiled when the spinner landed on the next question. "This is a three-part question—a really tough one," she said. "What do you call a group of rattlesnakes?"

"A rhumba," Ellie answered before anyone else could raise a hand.

"And group of toads?"

"A knot."

"And a group of dolphins?"

"A pod." Ellie was glad she knew so much about animals.

Mrs. Crispin nodded. "Excellent, Ellie!"

Ellie could feel the other girls staring at her again. She felt proud that she could answer the questions before anyone else—even Mrs. Crispin's extra-hard three-part question. She waited for the wheel to stop again.

"Who remembers how to spell and define *braggadocio*?" Mrs. Crispin asked.

Ellie was the first to spell that right. "It means boasting," she added. Mrs. Crispin smiled and sat down at her desk.

Then Mrs. Crispin gave them twenty minutes to start writing their autobiographies, which were due in a month.

Ellie liked this assignment, but she wasn't sure where to start. Before the hurricane? With her time at the shelters? She also wanted to write about the trip to Virginia in the Blue Goose. On the way, she and her mother had spent the night in a motel, and they had splurged on banana splits at the Granna Banana ice cream store nearby. And they had sung "The Wheels on the Truck Go Round and Round" at the top of their voices every time they crossed another state line.

She began to write the first sentence of her essay

in her very best cursive. She tried to make her capital *I* bow out nicely and her capital *S* twirl around— sort of like a treble clef on a sheet of music.

Ellie had just finished the first paragraph when she heard the sound of a piece of folded paper whisper to the floor by her desk. She thought it might be Hannah's essay, and she reached down to pick it up for her.

But it didn't look like an essay. The lined notebook paper was folded in a tiny little square, and it had Ellie's name printed on the front in block letters. Ellie opened the note and read:

How could someone who thinks she's so smart wear such prissy shoes?

She balled it up quickly.

But she didn't do it quickly enough.

Mrs. Crispin's voice roared out. "We don't pass notes in class at Twin Creeks," she said sternly, giving Chloe and Hannah each a detention slip without even asking who had passed it. Then she headed straight toward Ellie. "Give me that note right now."

Ellie could feel all the eyes in the classroom staring at her—yet again. She had to think fast. No matter what, she couldn't let anyone—not even Mrs. Crispin—know what the note said.

Just before Mrs. Crispin reached her desk, Ellie stuffed the paper in her mouth where she knew it would be safe from Mrs. Crispin's grasp. She heard someone in the front row gasp.

But Ellie knew that nothing Mrs. Crispin could say or do could hurt her any worse than the words she had read on that paper.

The words would start to smear in her throat and swirl into nothingness somewhere near her esophagus, and Mrs. Crispin would never know what someone had written.

That Ellie Taylor was wearing prissy-looking shoes.

Ellie looked down at those shoes all the way to the headmaster's office, with Mrs. Crispin marching behind her, scolding her at every step.

7

The headmaster, Mr. Flannery, motioned Ellie to a hard bench in the outer office. Then he ushered Mrs. Crispin into his private office and closed the door behind them. Ellie looked around, trying not to gawk at the hundred years of Twin Creeks history hanging in fancy frames on the wall or at the school secretary, who looked almost as old and mean as Mrs. Crispin herself.

Even with the door closed, Ellie could hear some of the words Mrs. Crispin was telling the headmaster.

DELIBERATELY DISOBEYED! Those were the ones that came out the loudest.

PUT IT IN HER MOUTH! Those came out pretty loud, too.

Mrs. Crispin huffed out of his office without even looking at Ellie.

"Come on in," Mr. Flannery said.

Ellie walked into his mahogany-paneled office and took a seat in a leather wing-back chair. She looked down at the floor, rubbing the toe of her shoe against a thick oriental rug. We Taylors are sturdy stock, she kept reminding herself, but somehow she didn't feel too sturdy sitting in that office under Mr. Flannery's stare.

"I hear you've had a *noteworthy* day," he said after a minute of silence.

Ellie looked up, surprised to see a semi-smile creep across his face. *Noteworthy*. She suddenly realized he was making a pun. He couldn't be all that angry if he was trying to make a joke. She wished *she* could think of something noteworthy to say, but nothing would come out.

"I've had to *eat my words* before, too." Mr. Flannery cleared his throat. "Not literally, of course."

It was another joke. Ellie was almost sure of it.

Mr. Flannery opened a folder in front of him.

"Elizabeth Ever Taylor. That's a pretty name."

"My mom named me after a movie star. I don't think people called her Ellie, though, like they call me."

"Yes. Elizabeth Taylor. One of my favorites," he said. "What about Ever? I've never known anyone named Ever before. Is that a family name?"

Ellie wasn't exactly sure what Mr. Flannery meant. Maybe he meant a name like McGregor or Kennedy—one of those first-last names she had heard in class.

Ellie nodded. "Sort of," she said. "My dad thought it up. He said I'd be the first person in his family *ever* to go to college. That maybe I'd be the first *ever* female chief justice of the Supreme Court. Or maybe even the first woman president *ever*. Mostly he just wanted me to be the best me *ever*. When I made a mistake, a really big one, that's what he'd always say to me."

Mr. Flannery shuffled through the folder labeled with Ellie's name.

"I saw from the material your mother sent us that you made a perfect score on your state test last year. And straight A's both in your old school and

the one you attended this fall. Excellent recommendations from your teachers. The admissions board found you worthy of a full scholarship." He paused and closed her folder. "We have put our faith in you, Ellie," he said. "I trust you'll never let something like this happen again."

Ellie nodded. She was trying hard not to cry.

"I can't even imagine living through a hurricane," he said kindly, changing the subject.

"We loaded up everything we could in the Blue Goose—that's our truck—and drove out of town where we'd be safe from the storm. We were supposed to meet up with my dad and our dog, but they never made it."

"Did you stay with relatives? Friends?"

"They all had their homes destroyed, too, but we were lucky in a way. We had to stay in a smelly shelter in a gym for just a month. Then we moved to a room of our own in a nice shelter. The hurricane left a lot of people homeless, but Mom said we weren't really homeless. We were just between homes for a while—it ended up only being four months."

"Your mother must be a very smart woman."

"Yes, sir. She didn't go to college, but that didn't keep her from getting smart on her own. Why, B.H., she worked as the head cook at Sally's Salty Dog. People came there from all over just to get some of my mother's famous potato salad."

"B.H.?"

"B.H. Before the Hurricane. Mom divides everything into Before the Hurricane and After the Hurricane. B.H. and A.H."

Mr. Flannery stood up and looked out the window. He cleared his throat again.

"And the hurricane washed Sally's Salty Dog away, too?"

Ellie nodded yes. "That's what they say, though I've never actually been back to see for myself."

"You've been through a lot, Ellie." He took off his wire-rimmed glasses and rubbed his left eye. "I can't imagine losing everything."

"We didn't lose everything, Mr. Flannery. A lot, maybe, but not everything. Mom says you can't count on anything you can touch lasting forever, anyway . . . not buildings, not people, not even pretty shoes."

Silence wrapped around the two of them—Mr.

Flannery still looking out the window, Ellie still rubbing the toe of her shoe on the patterned rug.

Mr. Flannery must have heard the soft shuffle her shoe was making. He looked down and stared at it. "Your shoes are beautiful."

"My dad bought them for me. But they're not regulation, are they?" Ellie asked, remembering what Mrs. Crispin had said.

Mr. Flannery thought for a minute. "Well, they're black. They're leather. They're not tennis shoes, and they don't have high heels. They may not be like the ones most students here wear, but I think we might be able to consider them regulation."

"So I can wear my shoes again tomorrow?"

"On one condition. If you'll write Mrs. Crispin a letter saying you're sorry you disobeyed her, I'll tell her you may wear the shoes."

Ellie wanted to say "okey dokey." Instead, she nodded yes. After a few seconds, she cocked her head to one side. "Do you think the other girls might be jealous because my shoes are so pretty?" she asked.

"Maybe. But maybe they're jealous because you're so smart."

Ellie couldn't imagine that anybody would be jealous because she was smart.

"I think it's my shoes," she said.

8

On the way from Mr. Flannery's office to Mrs. Crispin's class, Ellie could think of a few questions she'd like to ask her teacher.

Like, "What do you call a group of Twin Creeks girls?"

That one was easy, Ellie thought. Mr. Cook had been right. They were snobs.

Or, "What do you call a group of teachers like Mrs. Crispin?"

The thought of what she would like to answer almost made her laugh. A quiver, Ellie thought. Just like a quiver of cobras—ready to strike at any minute. Or a shiver. That's what you called a group of sharks. A shiver of Crispins would make any student shiver.

A few of the girls giggled when she walked by them and back to her desk. When Mrs. Crispin cleared her throat loudly, the giggles stopped. "We were just starting the word problems on page 182, Ellie," Mrs. Crispin said. Her voice didn't sound so angry anymore.

Ellie sat by herself at lunch. Then she went back to her classroom and wrote Mrs. Crispin the apology Mr. Flannery had asked her to write. Ellie said she was very, very sorry that she had put the note in her mouth and that she would never do a disrespectful or deliberately disobedient thing like that again. She underlined the "deliberately disobedient" part, but she didn't even try to make her handwriting look pretty this time.

Ellie sat by herself on the long bus ride home. As the bus chugged to a stop at one big house after another all over the county, she couldn't wait to get back to Hunters' Hill.

When there was only one other student left on the bus, Ellie heard a book bag drop onto the seat across the aisle.

"I'm Ann Randolph," the girl said.

Ellie wondered if that was her whole name or if

she had a double name like some of the other girls in her class.

"Ann Randolph Carter."

"I'm Ellie," Ellie said. "Ellie Taylor." Then she thought it might make a better impression if she had a double-sounding name, too. "Ellie Ever Taylor."

"New at TC?"

Ellie nodded.

"I didn't think I'd seen you around before. I was new last semester. I'm in fifth grade. How do you like it here?" Ann Randolph asked. She took an orange out of her backpack, peeled it, and handed Ellie a slice.

"Cool. It's cool."

"Mega," Ann Randolph corrected her. "Nobody at TC says 'cool' anymore. 'Cool' is so . . . so uncool now. Last semester we all said 'sweet' when we meant 'cool.' Now we all say 'mega' instead of 'sweet.' We say 'mega' when we mean 'very.' We say 'mega' all the time, even if we don't know exactly why we're saying it. It's a TC thing. You'll catch on." She ate another piece of orange. "Who's your teacher?"

"Mrs. Crispin."

"She's mega mean. Everybody says so. I'm glad I never had her."

The bus stopped at the entrance to Hunters' Hill. Ellie grabbed her stack of books—she didn't have a book bag yet—and started to get off.

"What a *mega* mansion!" Ann Randolph said, looking at the Hunters' house in the distance. She waved goodbye through the window and watched as Ellie punched in the code that would make the iron gates spring open.

Carpenters waved as Ellie trudged by. It took her almost ten minutes to walk from the road to the stables. But ten minutes wasn't enough time to figure out what to tell her mother about her first day at her new school.

She unlocked the door and climbed the stairs to her loft. She took off her patent leather flats and tucked them in the velvet shoe bag, tearing up at the thought of the "prissy shoes" note that had gotten her into such big trouble. Then she hung up her school uniform, wishing she never had to wear it again. The jeans and basset hound sweater she put on felt soft and comfortable and familiar.

Ellie didn't want to worry her mother. Maybe she could tell her that Mrs. Crispin knew a lot about animals and had introduced her personally to the headmaster. That would be sort of true. Before she left his office, Mr. Flannery told Ellie that he, too, had gotten off on the wrong foot with Mrs. Crispin on his first day as headmaster at Twin Creeks. She wanted to tell her mother that, but then she would have to explain about the hateful words the two jealous girls had written. She never wanted her mother to know about the note.

She heard the Blue Goose wheezing down the cobblestones toward the stables. Her mom looked tired when she came into their apartment, and Ellie could tell from her mother's face that her first day at school hadn't gone well, either.

"So how was your day?" Ellie asked before her mother could ask her the same question.

"I've got a bruise on my back where a colt kicked me. I got stepped on by an ornery pony, and I got burned on the bottom of my arm when I bumped into the Dragon. Other than that," she said, managing to laugh, "my day went just fine."

Then her face softened. "But don't worry about me, Ellie. Things will get better. Bad beginnings usually make for good endings anyway. How was your day?"

"Okay," Ellie said.

"Just okay?"

"Just okay," Ellie repeated. "We better feed the horses," she said, trying to change the subject.

They had let the horses out into their pasture that morning—it was still warm for winter—and Ellie watched them trot to her mother when she went to call them in for supper. She noticed that her mother was limping a little on her left leg as she walked. Ellie wondered if the horses would ever come to her the way they came to her mother.

Her mother had once told her that horses always know when someone is afraid of them. Maybe the girls at Twin Creeks could sense her fear.

Ellie helped her mom by wiping the water bowl in each stall with a clean rag. Sometimes she pushed the trigger on the bottom of the bowl, making the water flow over her fingers.

They took alfalfa and oats to Okey Dokey. After

that, Ellie watched her mother rub cream onto Pogo's burn, cringing at the sight of the hardening scab. Then she helped her mother mix the mash for Glory. The corn oil softened the bran, and she mixed in a dollop of molasses and a little grated carrot for flavoring. After she poured that from a pail into his trough, she broke cubes of alfalfa into bits, softened them with warm water, and hung them in a bucket by the hayrack.

The next morning, with a little help from her mother, Ellie ironed the blouse of her school uniform. Then she slipped into her patent leather shoes. How could anybody think those shoes were prissy-looking? They were beautiful! Could the headmaster have been right about the girls being jealous not of her shoes, but of her brain? Maybe she had shown off too much when Mrs. Crispin had asked her those questions. Her mother had said Twin Creeks was full of smart girls. Maybe those other smart girls thought she was full of *braggadocio*.

The bus arrived at school early, and Ellie headed toward the restroom. She didn't want to go to Mrs. Crispin's room any sooner than she had to, so she hid in one of the stalls for a long while, waiting for the warning bell to ring. Listening to other girls come and go, she thought she recognized Hannah's voice. Once Ellie was sure, she sat down on the toilet—the lid was closed—and lifted her feet up high enough to make sure Hannah didn't look under the stall door and see her "prissy" shoes.

Then she recognized McGregor's voice. "It's the truth!" McGregor said. "I heard from a fifth grader whose bus stop is near hers. That new girl's house is a mansion—a mega mansion—like something a president or at least a movie star would live in!"

"The President lives in the White House," Hannah said. "Besides, you have a big house, too."

Ellie heard the restroom door squeak open, then close again. More footsteps.

"The new girl's family is *mega, mega* rich," Ellie heard Hannah tell someone else. "Like a mega millionaire."

Ellie knew they must be talking about one of the other new girls. Mrs. Crispin had said there were three in the school. The bell rang, and Ellie heard their voices drift out into the hall.

When she walked into Mrs. Crispin's room just before the final bell, Ellie made sure to hold her head up extra high and square her shoulders.

9

After lunch, Ellie sat on her throne in the restroom again. She felt safe locked in there. Safe from the way the mega snobs in her class whispered when she walked by. Were they talking about her shoes again? Safe from their strange looks—she had caught several of them staring at her when she sat down for lunch. On her throne in the restroom, she wouldn't have to hear the thunder of Mrs. Crispin's sensible black shoes moving around the room.

Ellie had to admit that things had been better today. Not mega better. Just a little better. Some of the girls had actually been nice to her at lunch. Amanda Barton told her not to worry about old

Mrs. Crispin—that her mother had been in Mrs. Crispin's class twenty-five years ago, and she had lived to tell about it. Weesie Caldwell even said she really liked Ellie's patent leather shoes. But since Weesie had to wear ugly orthopedic shoes for her pigeon-toed feet, Ellie figured Weesie would like anyone else's shoes. And Stratford Bell said she liked them, too, but she wore shoes that looked like galoshes, and to make matters worse, she had scribbled smiley faces on the sides with Magic Marker. The girls who sat with her were clearly not mega popular.

By now, Ellie could recognize all their voices.

"I heard she was a *billionaire*," she heard Chloe say while she brushed her hair at the restroom sink.

They must be talking about that other new girl again, Ellie thought. She wondered what kind of shoes that new girl wore.

"I found out at lunch why the new girl's family is so rich, Chloe." Ellie could imagine Hannah shaking her hair as if to punctuate the words. "Her parents are *royalty*."

"You mean like a *king* and *queen*?" Ellie could tell Chloe didn't believe Hannah.

"Yep. Of some foreign country, but I forget which one," Hannah said knowingly.

"She doesn't look like a princess to me," Chloe said.

"I think she's really pretty—in a princess kind of way, I mean," whispered Hannah.

"And she doesn't act like a princess, either," Chloe said just before the bell rang for class. "Let's go."

As soon as the coast was clear, Ellie went to her classroom. She couldn't wait for school to be over. She wanted to tell her mother that a princess went to her school!

But her mother didn't seem to care. "Why don't you rub this on Pogo today?" she answered, handing Ellie the can of ointment.

During the morning bus ride on her third day at TC, Ellie sat by herself in the front seat. Earphones plugged into her ears, she listened to music while she finished her math homework. Once she was done, she kept her earphones on, but turned the music off to hear what people were saying. She hoped they were talking about the princess.

Hannah was sitting behind her, and Ellie heard her voice first.

"Just exactly how would you know?" she asked in a loud whisper. "Have you ever met a real princess before?"

Chloe admitted that she hadn't.

"She just doesn't want to be accused of"—Hannah stumbled on the word—"of bragga . . . braggadocio. Her parents sent her here to live with her nanny for a year so she could learn about America." She was whispering just loud enough for Ellie to hear.

"She seems to know a lot about America to be from another country," said Chloe.

Her whisper came out louder than a whisper should, and Hannah put her index finger to her lips to quiet her. "Shush," she said. "Somebody might hear you."

"Remember her answer about Jamestown?" Chloe asked in a voice so soft Ellie had to concentrate extra hard to make out her words. "And she even knew about that President Adams—James or John—I forget which," Chloe continued. "She talks like an American, though her accent is kind of different."

But *I* answered the question about President John Adams, Ellie thought. She suddenly realized they were talking about her—they thought *she* was a princess. Oh, no! How could they? Then she remembered what Ann Randolph had said when she got off the bus two days earlier. She must have assumed that Ellie's family lived in the mega mansion and started the rumor. Ellie kept on listening.

"She must have private tutors who are American," Hannah said.

"No wonder she's so smart. Any of us could be that smart if we had private tutors like she does," said Chloe. "Do you think she has a real crown?"

"I'm sure of it," said Hannah. "My mother was watching a program about kings and queens on the History Channel last week. They all wear crowns. I thought I recognized her the first time she walked into school—even without her crown."

"Why don't we just ask her if she's a princess?" suggested Chloe.

"It's not proper," Hannah said haughtily. "You

don't just go around asking a real princess a question like that. You're supposed to know."

"Can you keep a secret?" Ellie heard Chloe ask Schyler Ferguson.

"Of course I can," Schyler said.

"Ellie is a princess. A real princess!"

"Wouldn't a princess come to school in a limousine instead of a school bus, and wouldn't she have guards? I thought all royal families had lots of guards," Schyler said.

"Maybe her bodyguards follow the bus," said Chloe. "And didn't you see the man with a bow tie fixing the intercom in our room yesterday? I bet he was just pretending, and he's another one of her bodyguards."

"Can you believe it? A princess with bodyguards right in our own school," said Schyler.

Her? A princess? So smart because she had a private tutor? Ellie wanted to laugh at the absurdity of it all.

10

Ellie couldn't help but wonder what her life would be like if she really were a princess. Would people call her Princess Ellie? Or just Princess? Or just Ellie? Would she have to wear a tiara everywhere she went? Would she wear it to the bathroom? Would the tiara have diamonds or rubies or emeralds? Maybe all three? Would she wear her hair long, like Cinderella, or shorter, like Princess Diana? Ellie had seen old pictures of Princess Diana on television and thought she was beautiful. She wondered if Princess Diana had ever worn pretty, princess-y, prissy shoes like hers.

Everybody was nicer to her on the bus ride home that day. They didn't ask her about being a princess—that would have been mega rude, Ellie figured. But she could tell they had heard the rumor by the way they were acting.

She worried the rest of the afternoon about what she should do. She thought about it while she was tending to Pogo. While she was mixing corn oil into Glory's mash. While she was giving Hannibal head rubs and Buttermilk shoulder pats. She even talked about her problem to Raffles, who cocked her ears forward as if she really wanted to listen. The horses, too, were beginning to be nicer to her, even if she wasn't a princess.

Ellie knew that starting a rumor or even spreading one was wrong, but why should she deny a rumor that was clearly in her favor? After all, *she* hadn't started it. *She* hadn't spread it. And *she* certainly didn't believe it. If she hadn't been eavesdropping, she wouldn't even know about it.

She walked down to Okey Dokey's pasture. She knew better than to go near that horse, but her mother had given her permission to watch him from the other side of his fence. She leaned against the top rail. Nobody would find out who she really was, she thought as she watched Okey Dokey gallop across the pasture. Her mother was too busy learning to shoe horses to ever come to Ellie's school. They'd be buying a place of their own and maybe even moving away from Twin Creeks when her mother finished her apprenticeship. If they were going to move, what harm could the rumor possibly do?

The next day, Hannah wore a pair of black patent leather shoes just like Ellie's. The day after, Chloe had the same kind of shoes on. By Monday, Ellie counted five more pairs just like them in her class. By Tuesday, everyone wore them—except Weesie, who still had to wear her orthopedic shoes, and Stratford, who still liked to doodle on the sides of her sensible brown almost-leather galoshes-shoes. Ellie could tell that Mrs. Crispin preferred feet to be dressed in plain brown shoes, but she couldn't say anything. The day after Mrs. Crispin had marched Ellie to his office, Mr. Flannery had announced on the intercom that the girls could wear any kind of brown or black leather shoes—as long as they weren't tennis shoes and didn't have high heels.

Nobody had asked her if she was a princess— she was glad Hannah had seen to that. And nobody seemed jealous of her even if they did think she was mega smart and mega rich and mega royal. Maybe people made an exception for princesses, Ellie thought. The more the girls treated her like a princess, the more she began to feel like one.

Ellie felt that as long as everybody thought she was a princess, she might as well be good at it. She took turns eating with absolutely everybody at lunch, which was the only time the class didn't have to stay in alphabetical order. She chose Stratford first when she got to captain the soccer team at recess, even though she knew Stratford couldn't run very fast—especially with galoshes on. Nobody was surprised—not even Ellie—when Hannah nominated her for second semester's class president, with Chloe seconding the motion. Ellie would be running against McGregor and Schyler.

A *princess* for class *president*! Ellie thought as she helped her mother bring in the horses that night. She would never use that slogan, of course, but she laughed at the thought of it. She wished she could share the laugh with her mom, but she was pretty sure her mom wouldn't think Ellie's reign as a princess was funny. Instead, they walked silently down to Okey Dokey's pasture. He still ran away every time they came to give him food, as if he were playing tag and didn't want to be tagged. "You just have to be patient with him," her mother cautioned. "Everything in its own time."

While they coaxed the other horses into their stalls, Mrs. Taylor talked about the farrier who was teaching her the trade.

"He's almost as good a farrier as your father," she told Ellie. "And a lot more patient with me. I really like what I'm doing."

"Does he think you'll be good?"

"I think so. He says I'm learning fast. At first he just let me trim a horse's hooves—that's pretty easy to do if the horse is used to it. Today, I put on my first pair of shoes all by myself. Trimmed the hooves. Shaped the horseshoes just right. Hammered them on perfectly. Your father would have been proud."

"You haven't gotten any burns lately from the Dragon?" asked Ellie.

Her mother shook her head. "No more bruised

backs or lame feet for me lately," she said. "I'm getting better at it every day." She said it proudly, but she didn't sound full of braggadocio. "I've still got a lot to learn, but I know I can do it now. If I work hard enough, I really *can* be the other Taylor in Taylor-Made Horseshoes."

"And we won't be 'tweeners anymore?" Ellie asked.

"That's right," her mother said. "Houses are expensive around here, but I think we'll be able to afford something small when I get customers of my own."

"So you don't think we'll be moving out of town?"

"I'd hate to see you leave TC. It's such a good school, and you seem to be happy there," Mrs. Taylor said.

"What makes people snobs?" Ellie suddenly asked. She'd been wondering about that ever since she started at TC. Even though wearing uniforms was supposed to make all the girls at TC look the same, some still seemed to think they were better than others.

"Your father worked on a lot of horses owned by very rich people. He said the ones who had really made it to the top were almost always nice—real classy in an unsnobby way. I think snobs just pretend to be richer or more important than they know they actually are. They're bullies who beat other people up with mean words or haughty looks. Classy people would never act like that."

Mrs. Taylor coaxed Glory to eat by pouring more molasses into his oats. She put some mash in her hand and waited for Glory to gum at it.

"Anyway, Ellie, why do you ask? Have any of the girls at TC been snobby to you?"

"Maybe a little at first," Ellie admitted. "But not now. Why, I even got nominated to run for class president today."

Mrs. Taylor wiped the stickiness of the molasses from her fingers onto her jeans before hugging Ellie. "My daughter, the president. Ellie *Ever* and all that," she said. "I told you that not all those girls could be snobs. I knew you'd fit in just fine."

When her mom brushed Ellie's hair away from her eyes, Ellie noticed how bruised and scarred her hands were. If only her mother really were a queen, her hands could be soft and her nails could be long and smooth and have pink polish on them.

Though she could still almost hear his voice, she couldn't remember what her father's hands looked like anymore. But Ellie could still touch her mother's hands. She went to the tack room and found a can of sweet-smelling salve. Then she made her mother sit down on the steps and slathered it on her mother's banged-up fingers.

11

Ellie wrote her campaign speech that night and read it first to Pogo, then to her mother. Her mother clapped loudly, the way Ellie knew she would. "Your ideas are great, Ellie, but shouldn't the class be doing something to help others?"

Ellie knew just the thing to suggest. She added that something to her speech before she went to bed. She worked on her speech some more on the bus ride and even more during lunch.

"McGregor has been class president forever," Hannah told Ellie, offering her one of her cookies at lunch. "Mrs. Cameron's first grade, Mrs. Hurst's second grade, and Mr. Larson's third grade, and first semester of the fourth grade. We need a change."

Ellie broke off a piece of roll, the best part of the cafeteria food. She nibbled at it gracefully, the way she thought a princess should.

"Don't worry about McGregor," Chloe told her between spoonfuls of vegetable soup. "She makes the same big suggestions every year—and none of her ideas ever happen."

"I'd rather suggest small changes first," Ellie said. "If you promise people something, you ought to do it." Ellie thought that sounded like something a real princess would say.

"Promise me you'll suggest that all fourth graders get extra recess time," said Kennedy. She loved to play soccer at recess.

Ellie knew Mrs. Crispin thought even fifteen minutes of recess was a waste of time. She knew better than to make that promise.

"You could promise more time for art," suggested Stratford. Ellie thought she might be running out of doodling room on her galoshes.

Samantha Cantrell wanted more time for

chorus; she had the prettiest voice in the school and always got to sing the solos.

Right after lunch, it was time for the campaign speeches and the election. "The nominees can speak for no more than three minutes each," Mrs. Crispin said, "and they'll speak in alphabetical order—McGregor Adams, then Schyler Ferguson, and finally Ellie Taylor."

McGregor walked to the podium. "I'm the most experienced person on the ballot," she began, "and experience is what counts in this election. I've had three and a half years learning how to lead our class to new heights. I know how to get things done around here. I will listen to your suggestions. Remember that a vote for McGregor Adams is a vote for yourself, too." The class applauded politely.

"Schyler, it's your turn." Mrs. Crispin motioned her to the podium.

"Now is a time for change at TC," Schyler began. "My father is chairman of the board of directors, and I will personally ask him to get rid of our ugly school uniforms if you elect me. I already have something really cute in mind. Or maybe I can get rid of our uniforms altogether so we can each wear what we want. Now that is really a *mega* great idea!"

Ellie thought the applause was louder for Schyler than for McGregor. When it was Ellie's turn at the podium, she remembered to stand up straight and hold her head proudly.

"I can't promise you my ideas will work, but if you elect me, I'll suggest this to Mrs. Crispin: that anyone who has her homework done on time all week can choose a treat for herself on Friday afternoon," Ellie began. The teacher at her school B.H. had let them do that, and it made everybody work harder. "And I'll suggest that a person could choose to play soccer or paint or sing." Ellie saw smiles from Kennedy and Stratford and Samantha. Out of the corner of her eye, she thought she could even see Mrs. Crispin nodding in agreement.

"And I'd want to appoint someone different every week to serve as my assistant." Ellie thought that was fair. "Then the class can vote on who has worked the hardest at the job, and that person can be president for the last month of school.

"I would be happy to help that person out as President Emeritus." Ellie knew that term was Latin for an honorary title held after a person retires, and she thought it sounded like a term a princess—a *really smart* princess with an American tutor—would know.

"And most important," Ellie proposed, "I want to help people in homeless shelters—by giving them something they need and maybe something they just want. Nothing old or worn out. Nothing broken or banged up. Something brand-new and beautiful."

"It must be awful to have as little as those people have," Victoria Davis said when Ellie suggested that. "Imagine not even being able to buy any new clothes! No one I know is that poor."

Ellie felt her throat lump, but she drew herself up and spoke in her most princess-like, most presidential voice. She knew that she could never admit to having lived in a shelter—she was sure no princess had ever done that.

Instead she said, "I have done some research on homelessness." She guessed living in a shelter counted as research. "These days, lots and lots of people are"—Ellie paused, remembering her mother's words—"between homes. Some have lost their jobs. Some are too sick to work anymore. Some have lost their houses in natural disasters—like hurricanes or tornadoes or fires or floods or earthquakes. Things like that can happen to anybody, and I think we should do what we can to help . . . those people." The class broke into loud applause after she finished her speech.

Ellie was elected class president in a landslide. She knew it was a landslide because Hannah told her so. Hannah had peeked when Mrs. Crispin had told them to close their eyes for the hands-up voting; she said McGregor and Schyler each just got one vote apiece—her own.

"That speech could've gotten you elected president of the United States," Hannah told her after the election. Ellie thought that being president of the United States might even be better than being a princess.

"I especially liked what you said about the homeless," Mrs. Crispin whispered to Ellie.

Ellie had a moment of panic. Did Mrs. Crispin

know about her past? Would she tell the class that Ellie herself had been one of "those people"?

But Ellie's worries subsided when Mrs. Cripsin sent Ellie to the library to get a copy of *Bulfinch's Mythology*. It was her first official act as class president.

12

After the election, Ellie was determined not to be afraid of Mrs. Crispin anymore. In a strange sort of way, she was beginning to like her teacher.

Mrs. Crispin seemed to enjoy playing a game with Ellie when she came in each morning. She would try to stump Ellie by naming some kind of mammal or bird or reptile nobody had ever heard of—like a ptarmigan, for example—just to see if Ellie knew what a group of them was called.

"A covey," Ellie had shot back even though she didn't really know what a ptarmigan was, though she thought it was a kind of bird. Ellie was glad she had read about animals on those afternoons when she had nothing else to do at the shelter.

Mrs. Crispin had almost stumped Ellie once when she asked her what one called a group of cats. She had answered clowder. Mrs. Crispin said it was a clutter of cats. She seemed excited that she had finally gotten the best of Ellie. But when Mrs. Crispin looked it up, she had to admit that both *clowder* and *clutter* were right.

With so many people wanting to sit next to her on the bus, Ellie found it harder to eavesdrop while pretending to listen to music through her earphones. But the day after the election, she spread her book bag out over the other half of her seat and acted busy reading when her friends walked by. She turned the music off when the bus turned onto the back roads.

She heard Stratford's tiny voice first. "I'm glad Ellie won," she told McGregor.

Ellie could hardly believe that Stratford had the nerve to stand up to McGregor!

"She wouldn't have won if she weren't a princess," McGregor said.

"Yes, she would have," said Stratford. "Even if she weren't a princess. Because Ellie Taylor makes everybody feel like somebody special. That's why I voted for her. That's why everybody except you and Schyler did."

McGregor's patent leather ballet shoes with the bows clicked hard against the floor of the bus. Ellie still couldn't imagine little Stratford in her galoshes talking like that to McGregor. Ellie was so stunned she was afraid she might gasp out loud. Then everybody would realize that she had been eavesdropping.

Ellie heard Hannah talking about a birthday party. Her own birthday was coming up in a few days. She wondered who else had one, too. She hadn't been invited to the birthday party they were talking about. Probably someone she didn't know. Someone who didn't go to Twin Creeks.

She heard Kennedy's voice next. "I can't wait till the party on Saturday," she said. "I even canceled my music lesson so I could go. I hope Ellie doesn't find out about it. It would ruin the surprise."

Ellie gripped the side of her seat. A surprise party for her? Where?

"Everybody's dying to see where she lives," Kennedy said. "Everybody says her house is enormous. We'll probably get to ride her horses if it's not too cold. I sure hope it doesn't snow this weekend."

"It was mega nice the way her mother had Mrs. Crispin invite absolutely everybody," Stratford said.

"Mrs. Crispin sure fooled Ellie. That was great how she sent her to the library so she could tell everybody about the party." Ellie heard Hannah's laugh.

"Maybe we should all bring something for our homeless project in addition to her birthday presents," suggested Chloe. "I bet Ellie would really like that."

"Great idea! I'll tell everyone else," said Hannah.

Suddenly Ellie felt herself swimming in panic. What was going to happen when the other girls discovered she was not a princess at all? Would they still like her when they found out she was a girl a hateful hurricane had left homeless—like some of the people their project was going to help?

Ellie realized she was about to lose her tiara.

She had to think of something. And quick.

She tried to act like nothing was wrong at school. But it was hard to focus on the ancient world of gods and heroes in *Bulfinch's Mythology* when she knew her own world was about to fall apart.

On Thursday night, Ellie thought about her problem. First, she decided to call Mrs. Crispin, disguise her voice to sound like a grownup's, and tell her to announce that the birthday party had to be canceled because of a family emergency.

But then what would her mother think when nobody showed up for the surprise party? That Mrs. Crispin had given everybody the wrong address? Mrs. Crispin didn't make mistakes like that—certainly not something as important as the address to someone's birthday party.

That nobody liked Ellie enough to come—that's what her mother would think.

And Ellie knew thinking that would wrinkle her mother's heart!

Then she thought she could pretend to be sick. Maybe she could put the thermometer under hot water so it would read really high when she showed it to her mother. Her father said that had worked for him once when he didn't want to go to school. If she could convince her mother that she had a really high fever—maybe something highly contagious—she'd have to cancel the party.

But then she would just postpone it until Ellie got well.

Ellie sat down at her desk and flicked on the lamp. A sheet of notebook paper stared back at her.

The next day was Ellie's turn to read her autobiography to the class, and she had been working on it all month. Last week, she had thought it was her best essay ever. But somehow the words that had seemed so good then didn't seem so good anymore. It was full of countries she had never visited and people she had never met and animals she had never petted. Lots of big words. Perfect grammar. Even the handwriting was pretty good.

An essay fit for a princess!

Only Ellie wasn't a princess. If she were, then her mother wouldn't have scarred hands, and the governor wouldn't have called her father a true American hero. She might not even know how it felt when your heart got wrinkled.

Ellie lay in bed worrying most of the night. What should she to do? Was it better to be accepted for who they all thought she was? Or to be herself

and risk not being accepted at all? Was it better to have the other girls at TC think she was a princess, or admit to being a pauper in prissy patent leather shoes? Ellie had so wanted to be a princess that she hadn't even thought about what Mrs. Crispin might have said if she had read her Princess Ellie essay. From Mrs. Crispin's comment about Ellie's class project idea, Ellie felt sure that she knew the truth. Was it time for everybody else to know, too?

Could she, would she, ever be brave enough to be just the best Ellie *Ever* again?

Nothing more. Nothing less, either. Just the best Ellie *Ever*.

13

Ellie got up early to redo her autobiography and hurried to finish it before she caught the bus. She wrote about B.H. and A.H. She wrote about waking up on Christmas Day in Noah's Ark and the surprise of moving to the apartment where Mr. Hunter had let them live near his stables. She wrote about how her mother was learning to be a farrier like her father, who was a true American hero. And how when her mother got to be a real farrier, she would make enough money to buy them a new house, and they wouldn't be 'tweeners anymore.

She wrote about how they honked the horn on the Blue Goose and sang "The Wheels on the Truck" every time they crossed another state line. She wrote about splurging on banana splits at Granna Banana.

She even wrote about how, what seemed like a long time ago, her father had bought her a pair of black patent leather shoes. Pretty, princess-y, *prissy* ballet flats.

Writing the introduction to her autobiography was the hardest part for Ellie, and she wrote it last. For her, it was the most important part, and she had to say things just right. She crossed out almost as many words as she left on the paper.

Mrs. Crispin started the day with the reading of autobiographies.

Ellie remembered to pinch the slouchiness out of her shoulders as she walked to the front of the room. And to hold her chin high.

The way a princess would.

A Taylor-Made Princess.

"I wrote something I'd like to read before I read my autobiography," Ellie began. "Sort of an intro-duction." She cleared her throat and began.

"Even though we never talked about it, I know from overhearing your conversations that you all think I'm a princess and are expecting me to tell you how I live, how a princess lives," Ellie said. "And the first essay I wrote did describe all of that, but the only crown I ever wore was a cardboard one I got at Burger King."

Ellie cleared her throat again, then continued reading. "I wanted to make friends here. I didn't want to be a misfit . . . a misfit like the horses Mr. Hunter rescued and brought to the farm where we live. Those horses are old and lame and foundered and abused and scarred and scared and forgotten. But they remind me every day how important it is to care about every living thing, even if—*especially* if—they can't do anything for you in return."

She turned to the next page of her introduction.

"I wanted to be a winner like the horses who used to live at the stable next to where my mother and I live," Ellie read. "So I pretended to be the winner you wanted me to be. But it was wrong to pretend." She paused again, running her eyes up and down the rows.

"Because, as my mom says, a person can lose almost everything else, and be okay," Ellie ended, "but if she loses *herself*, she loses *everything*." She laid her paper down on the podium.

"I'm sorry I ever let you think I was a princess," she said. "That was a mistake. If my father were here, he would have reminded me that all I ever needed to be was the best Ellie *Ever*. Not some princess people liked because of what they thought I had. Just the best Ellie *Ever*." Ellie paused again, trying to choke back tears. "For him, that would have been more than enough." She glanced at everyone in the room, then locked eyes with Mrs. Crispin. "Now I'd like to read to you about my real life."

Ellie looked out over the sea of faces in the classroom as she read, seeing that her honesty was stunning them all. She even thought that Hannah looked ashamed when she got to the part about the black patent leather ballet shoes.

The other fifteen girls in the room were still stunned when Ellie finished reading her autobiography and took her seat.

Mrs. Crispin broke the silence. "I can't believe anybody thought you were a princess," she said.

"I can't understand why anybody would think I was a princess, either," said Ellie.

"That's how silly rumors can be, how quickly they can get out of hand. The girls here have started a lot of rumors in the past, but I've never heard of one quite like this before. I wish I could have stopped it, but I'm usually the last to know about things. I didn't tell the other girls about your background because I wanted to respect your privacy, and I just didn't think it mattered anyway."

"It wasn't your fault. It was mine," Ellie said. "I should have stopped it."

Ellie somehow knew what Mrs. Crispin wanted to tell her: that everything would be just fine; that everybody would show up for her surprise birthday party; and that nobody would care where she had come from—just where she was going. But Ellie knew Mrs. Crispin wouldn't lie.

Ellie wanted to hug Mrs. Crispin, to tell her she was sure this was the day Okey Dokey would come right to her. That somebody had found her dog, Pandy, in time for Ellie's birthday. She wanted to say all those things, but she wouldn't lie, either.

She wouldn't lie, and she wouldn't pretend.

Not now. Not ever again.

On the morning of her birthday, Ellie woke up late to the smell of chocolate. Probably the frosting for her birthday cake. Then she heard the sound of scraping. Probably her mother peeling potatoes for her famous potato salad. Lots of scraping meant lots of potato salad nobody would show up to eat at her surprise birthday lunch. How would she explain to her mother why nobody came to a surprise birthday party she wasn't even supposed to know about?

Ellie stayed in bed, trying to figure out why she was so sure nobody would come. She hadn't really betrayed anybody, or even lied to them. The other girls had made up the rumors; *she* hadn't. She figured some of them, the really snobby ones, couldn't be bothered with someone like her who was different, who had been homeless, who didn't know or want to play by their rules. Scratch them and you'd sniff a snob, Mr. Cook had said.

But what had her mother meant by "Sniff a snob, and you'll get a whiff of scared"? Scared of what? What could the snobs possibly be scared of? Ellie still couldn't figure that out.

She was the smartest, and she was the poorest. Ellie realized she had two strikes against her at Twin Creeks. She couldn't help but be a misfit. Just like Glory and Buttermilk and Pogo and Hannibal and Raffles and Okey Dokey. Only she didn't have someone like Mr. Beckwith or Mr. Hunter to rescue her this time. She'd have to figure out a way to rescue herself.

She thought about Mr. Hunter again. What did he look like? Would he invite her to the big house when he returned in the spring? What had he thought of the thank-you note she and her mother had written him? Why did he do nice things for people he didn't even know? For unwanted horses?

She pulled on her jeans and basset hound

sweater and some old boots. "Would you mind feeding Okey Dokey this morning, Ellie?" she heard her mother call. "I've got some things to do around the house."

"But you told me not to go near him."

"It's your birthday. You're older now, and I've seen how good you are with horses. But be careful. I still want you to keep a distance."

"I'll go," Ellie said.

In the feed room, she ladled oats into a bucket and threw hay in the burlap bag. Then she went back into their apartment to grab a carrot. She walked to Okey Dokey's pasture and watched him at a distance for a long time. When she left the food in his shed and turned away, she could somehow feel the mustang looking at her, sizing her up from across the pasture. She walked back and climbed onto the top rung of the fence. Bracing herself against the cold, Ellie sat there, willing the horse to trust her. "Okey Dokey," she yelled, loud at first. "Come on up here." He didn't move. Then Ellie tried to say the words exactly the way her father used to say them. "Okey Dokey. Everything's going to be okey dokey."

Ellie would have given anything to hear her father say those words just one more time.

The horse came nearer, but not near enough to see her wrinkled heart. Maybe he would come that close later, when he realized he could trust her, when he was ready. Everything in its time.

Ellie walked back toward the stable. She heard a horse's whinny—it sounded like Hannibal's. Then she heard a whinny coming from Okey Dokey's pasture. She had never heard him whinny, and she loved the sound of it. When she turned into the feed room, Ellie heard another sound: scampering feet and the almost-stifled giggles of girls.

When she looked around the corner into the stable, Ellie heard the giggles again, and she could tell they were coming from the last stall. The heads of the gigglers were hidden by the top of the closed stall door, but Ellie could see shoes through the crack at the bottom of the lower one.

Lots of shoes.

Galoshes-looking shoes with smiley faces drawn in Magic Marker; ugly brown orthopedic shoes fancied up with pink laces; two pairs of loafers; four pairs of black patent leather ballet flats with

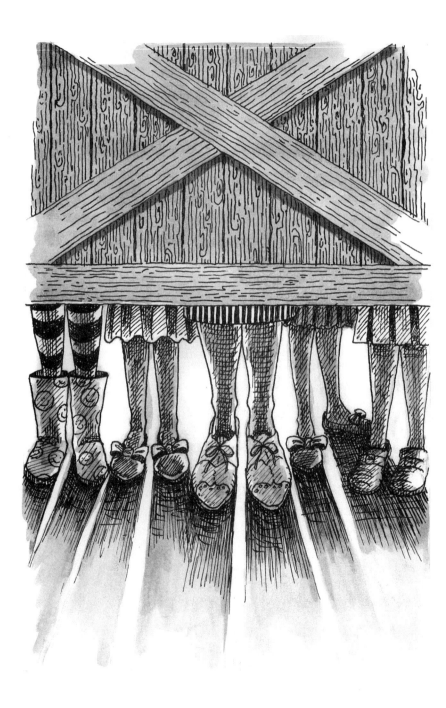

bows—pretty, prissy, *princess*-y shoes just like Ellie's father had bought her in that boutique.

Not all the girls in her class were there, but sixteen shoes meant eight were . . . the ones who liked her not for what she *had*, but for who she *was*. Who she *really* was! Then she saw one more pair of shoes. They were much larger—black, sensible shoes—exactly like the kind Mrs. Crispin always wore.

Even before the gigglers could jump out and yell "Surprise!" Ellie knew all those shoes were telling her that things *would* be okey dokey again.

She would have the best birthday.

Because she was the best Ellie.

The best Ellie *Ever*!